THE CASE OF THE
DISAPPEARING UNDERPANTS

THE MYSTERY OF THE
DISAPPEARING
UNDERPANTS

BY

NIKKI YOUNG

ILLUSTRATED BY MADDY BENNETT

STORYMAKERS PRESS

First published in Great Britain by Troubador Publishing in 2017

This edition published in Great Britain by Storymakers Press in 2021

Copyright © Nicola Young 2021

The moral right of the author has been asserted

A CIP catalogue for this book is available from the British Library.

ISBN 978-1-8384687-2-9

Typeset in 11pt Aldine401 BT

Storymakers Press
Kent, England, United Kingdom
Website: www.storymakerspress.com

To Hope, Scarlett & Ike

Have you ever had something lucky?

A pair of trainers that helped you run faster, a pen that made you have the best ideas, a hat that every time you wore it you won at chess?

Well I have my lucky underpants.

At least I did until they went missing.

Right when I needed them most.

It was last summer, when I started a secret agency with my friend James. We called it Trinity Spies, after our street, which is called Trinity Grove. I know Trinity means 'three' and there were only two of us, but we ended up with my next-door neighbour Stacey joining, so it did kind of make sense in the end.

This was the agency:

1. Me – Harry Bond, Agent 009 (my age). My real name is Harry Smith, but it's way too boring for a secret agent.
2. Brosnan – my black labradoodle dog.

If you didn't know, a labradoodle is cross between a labrador and a poodle. This makes for one crazy dog, but crazy in a good way. And yes, in case you were wondering about his name, we're all big James Bond fans in our house and Pierce Brosnan is my mum's favourite Bond actor. My dad wanted Connery, but someone told him all the best dogs have a name beginning with 'B', so Brosnan it was.

3. James Murphy – Agent James Hunt (inspired by the film *Mission Impossible*).

    James (also aged 9) is my best friend. We play football together and go to the same school. We're both sports mad but we don't like the other one to win. James is worse than me, though. He keeps a record of everything, like how many goals we've each scored, our best times for the 100 metres, how many tennis matches we've each won, etc., etc. That might sound annoying, but it's not. James is really funny and he makes me laugh a lot. And even better, he lives on the same street as me, so we get to see each other whenever we want.

4. Stacey Webster – Agent Stacey Cortez (because she wants to be like Carmen Cortez from the *Spy Kids* films, even though she looks nothing like her – Stacey has short-ish blond hair and is a bit like a pixie).

    Stacey wasn't in the secret agency to begin with, but because she's my next-door neighbour and kept interfering in our business all the time, she ended up being part of the team. I think it might have been because James quite likes her, although he would never say it. In the end, even I had to admit it was quite useful having her around.

This is the story of what happened during the summer. As leader, most of it is written by me, but I've included James' and Stacey's side of things as well, so that nothing is left out.

There were spy tricks, foxes and the mystery of the strange new people who moved into number 35 on our street. It kept the Trinity Spies very busy and it all started when my lucky underpants went missing…

PART 1

Week 1
Forming the Trinity Spies

We started the secret agency today – the first day of the first week of the school summer holidays. Our first job was to make a secret lookout den in my back garden (in the shed), where we are going to have our meetings. The shed was full of cobwebs and stank of the stuff Dad uses to paint the fence. We found an old plastic table and some chairs in there, so we spent most of the afternoon clearing a space so we could set them up. James got a bit fed up of doing that. He said it was boring (he always says stuff is boring).

'I'm going to go and find my lucky underpants,' I said to James. 'I think we might need them.'

'Gross, do you still wear those old things?' James said.

'You know I do.'

'Well I'm going home anyway. I'll come back tomorrow after breakfast.'

'Zero nine hundred hours for the meeting,' I said.

'Yeah, yeah, whatever,' he said as he walked out of the back garden gate.

James thought I only wore my lucky underpants for

football matches. What he didn't know is that I wore them when I played against him on the PlayStation, at table tennis club or even for a game of chess. Every time I had on my lucky underpants, I beat him and I knew I would need them to help me be the best secret agent.

But when I went up to my room disaster struck. They weren't in the back of my pants drawer, where I always keep them.

'Mum have you seen my lucky underpants?'

'Lucky underpants? Which ones are thcy?'

'The ones with Spiderman on them,' I called out, then immediately regretted it.

'Spiderman!' said my brother Max as he came out of his room. 'That's so lame.'

He ruffled my hair as he walked past, laughing all the way down the stairs. I felt like my face was on fire; no doubt, I would never live that down. Max, being fourteen, thinks he's a grown-up man already. Everything I do is lame according to him. I tried to rearrange my already messy curls.

'Mum, I need those pants. I have to wear them for the pre-season cup at the end of the holidays and for the football camps.'

'Well, I'm sure they're around somewhere. Knowing you, you've probably not looked properly and anyway that room of yours is so messy I'm surprised you can find anything. I'm always telling you to tidy it up.'

I could tell my mum was going to be no help whatsoever, so I went and checked in the laundry basket before going back to my room. I checked everywhere I could think of – my drawers, football bag, under the bed – but I couldn't find them. I sat down on the bed scratching my head.

'What am I going to do now, Brosnan?'

Brosnan gazed at me with his big black eyes and nuzzled his head into my lap. I always felt like he understood. He was the only one who seemed bothered by what had happened to me.

'If I don't find them in time for the cup game, I could risk our team losing. They've never lost a match when I've worn those pants and it will be my fault.'

I felt sick at the thought and couldn't help wondering how I would ever manage to beat James again if I didn't have those pants. I didn't move from my spot on the bed until Mum called up to say dinner was ready. After dinner, Brosnan and I went back out to the den, so we could keep up the watch duty, should anything happen. We hadn't been there long when we heard the back gate click open.

'Shush, Brosnan,' I said, 'someone's coming into the garden. It might be a thief who's come to hide his stash here where he thinks no one will find it.'

But then I heard:

'Harry… Harry… Oh, hello, what are you doing in there? And why are you wearing those stupid sunglasses when it's so dark?'

It was Stacey from next door (ugh!):

1. She never waits to be invited, just walks right in whenever she feels like it.
2. She asks way too many questions.
3. She's a girl and there's no way I was telling her about the secret agency. NO GIRLS ALLOWED.

So I pulled off my glasses and quickly shoved them under my seat.

'What do you want, Stacey?' I said to her.

'My mum sent me round to find out if you've had anything go missing from your washing line recently. We've had a T-shirt and a pillow case snatched. It's a bit of a mystery.'

MYSTERY

Both mine and Brosnan's ears pricked up as she said this.

A mystery washing thief. That could only mean one thing.

SOMEONE MUST HAVE STOLEN
MY LUCKY UNDERPANTS.

'No idea, but I'll let Mum know,' was all I said to Stacey, as I ran off.

TUESDAY

Today James came round early: 8:45 a.m., to be precise. He came in through the back gate and straight into the kitchen, like he always does. He doesn't need to knock; everyone is used to him being around. When I walked into the kitchen, he was sitting at the table eating a bowl of cereal, looking like he'd been up and dressed for ages. Even his hair was all styled in that sticky-up way he likes to do it.

'You not ready yet?' he said, through a mouthful of cornflakes.

I looked down at my worn tracksuit bottoms with the hole at the knee and thought about my messy curls that I could never be bothered to brush. This was typical of James. Because I told him to be here at 9:00 a.m., he made sure he was here earlier just so he could beat me. No doubt he would give himself a tick for winner of who gets to the meeting first. My stomach felt sick and heavy at the thought of my missing underpants.

'Have you not had breakfast yet?' I asked, sitting down opposite him and emptying what was left of the Rice Krispies (in other words, the dust at the bottom of the pack) into another bowl. As I poured the milk in, some of it bounced straight out of the bowl and landed on the table. I wiped it up with my sleeve.

'Yeah, this is my second breakfast. I got starving waiting around for you.' James got up to put his bowl in the sink, whilst I set about eating as fast as I could to catch him up.

'Whatever, James, come on, let's go have our meeting,' I said, as I slurped the last of the milk from the bowl and left it on the table.

At the agency headquarters, I told James all about the washing thief and we worked out our plan. First, we decided to investigate the neighbours – and I do have some interesting ones. I'll tell you about them.

Mrs O'Connor next door (the other side to Stacey) is from Ireland and she goes to church every day. My mum tries to avoid her when we are going to school because she talks so much it makes us late. She always gives me 50p when I see her, though, so I like her a lot.

Mrs O'Connor told us that she was missing one of her underskirts (gross!), so she couldn't be the thief.

Next door to her is grumpy old Mr Newsome, 'Gruesome Newsome' we call him (not to his face though). If we're playing football outside my house and the ball goes into his garden, he won't let us have it back. He's always shouting at us, saying we're too noisy, and he goes round to complain to Mum and Dad that we're out too late at night. None of us likes him.

We couldn't decide whether to knock on his door, but eventually we did.

'What do you want? I'm busy,' was his greeting.

Then, 'Stop wasting my time with such stupid questions. Be off with you before I call the police,' was his answer when we asked if he'd had any washing stolen.

'Seems like he's got something to hide to me,' said James.

I agreed.

Through the gate at the bottom of my garden is an alleyway that runs along the back of all the houses on our side of the street. In the afternoon we borrowed my dad's binoculars and went down to see if we could spy into Gruesome Newsome's garden, but his gate was locked and we couldn't see over his fence. We tried standing on a plastic crate to see over, but that didn't work either. Gruesome Newsome has the highest fence on the whole street and loads of trees at the bottom of his garden. Even with James balancing on my shoulders, it didn't help. And we were too wobbly like that anyway, so he couldn't even hold the binoculars straight to look through them. Instead, we went back to my house to see if we could get a better view from my bedroom window.

That was when we saw him hanging out some washing.

And not all of the clothes were his.

'There's a T-shirt that could be Stacey's,' I pointed out, 'but I can't see my lucky underpants.'

'Does that look like Mrs O'Connor's' underskirt?' said James.

We'd never seen Mrs O'Connor's underskirt before so we weren't sure, but we were pretty sure that Gruesome Newsome lived alone, so the question was why would he have clothes on his washing line that were definitely not his.

We set our task for the next day – to find out what Gruesome Newsome was up to.

'If I had my lucky underpants I bet we'd have found out who the thief is by now,' I said to Brosnan that night. 'But if the thief is wearing my lucky underpants, then we might never catch him.'

I rushed out the kitchen door and down the garden path at 8:40 a.m. this morning, only to find James already sitting in the lookout den. Another tick for James then, I thought, trying to put my missing lucky underpants to the back of my mind.

After what we'd seen yesterday, James and I decided we should investigate Gruesome Newsome, so we kicked a ball around in the street out the front of my house and waited for him to leave. When he came out of his house it didn't take him long to spot us.

'Oi, you young hooligans, you better not kick that ball into my rose bushes again or you'll be for it, do you hear?'

'Yes, Mr Newsome,' we said, as though we were answering a teacher at school.

We pretended to carry on playing, but as Gruesome Newsome began to walk off down the street we ran up to my front door and threw the ball into the house. Then we legged it back onto the street so we could follow him, ignoring the shout of 'watch it, lame boy,' from my brother, who happened to be walking through the hall at the same time and got hit on the ankles with the ball.

Gruesome Newsome was carrying a big bag and he took it to a house on Feather Street (that's two streets along from ours). We hid behind lamp posts, trees and bushes all the way in case he turned around and saw us, but he never did. I think he's probably a bit deaf, 'cause he's quite old. It was so funny. There's no way we could hide or camouflage ourselves and if he had turned around he would have easily seen us. When Gruesome Newsome went into the house, we waited behind a car parked opposite. We were waiting for ages, just sitting on the floor and James got bored, so we started playing 'throw the stone at the ant' to pass the time. We got so into it (especially James, of course) that we nearly missed Gruesome Newsome leaving. Luckily, I heard the front door bang shut and nudged James in the ribs to let him know. We watched Gruesome Newsome leave and this time he was carrying a different bag. Through the binoculars we saw an old woman in the house, taking the things out of the bag that Gruesome Newsome had brought. They looked like the clothes from his washing line, including Mrs O'Connor's underskirt (we thought).

WAS HE STEALING PEOPLE'S WASHING TO GIVE TO THIS OLD WOMAN?

I went to James' house today. He said it wasn't fair that he always had to come round to mine. I didn't mind and it was good to get away from Max, who was still winding me up about the Spiderman pants.

We went back to the old lady's house on Feather Street. James knocked on her door and said we were investigating the disappearance of washing from people's lines and had she lost any of her own? I would have knocked on her door, but James really wanted to do it.

'I don't know, young man. I'll have to ask my Colin. He's the one who does all my washing for me,' the old lady said.

Then she invited us in! It was awful. We thought we'd never get out of there.

1. Old people talk a lot.
2. Their houses smell funny.
3. They have nice biscuits though.

But we did learn something: 'Colin' is Gruesome Newsome and the old lady is his mum!

We saw lots of funny pictures of him when he was a boy. She even let us keep one of them. James said he was going to use it to bribe Gruesome Newsome next time he wouldn't let us have our ball back. He said we could threaten to stick posters of him all over the street for everyone to laugh at. I'm not sure if Gruesome Newsome would care about that really, but it would be worth a try. One thing we were sure of is Gruesome Newsome was not the thief.

AND IF HE WASN'T THE THIEF, THEN WHO WAS?

After doing some more digging around, which meant asking more of the neighbours if they'd had any washing stolen from their lines, we found out that only me, Stacey and Mrs O'Connor had had clothes taken.

'So, we're looking for someone dressed in an underskirt, T-shirt and possibly my underpants, whilst carrying a pillow case,' I said to James.

We thought, based on the evidence we'd found, that the thief must be close by, so we searched around the three gardens for clues (luckily, Stacey was out all day today so she didn't interfere). This is what we found:

1. A punctured old football (mine).
2. A chewed up old trainer (possibly Stacey's).
3. Loads of tennis balls (probably mine).
4. A rusty old watering can (Mrs O'Connor's).

This was all very interesting but it wasn't getting us closer to finding the thief. That was, until James found something VERY interesting: some pegs. There was one on our side of the garden and another on Mrs O'Connor's side. There's no fence between our two gardens, just a huge deep hedge.

'The thief?'

'In there.'

James and I spoke at the same time, pointing to the hedge.

'We need to tempt him out,' I said. 'We can hide in the lookout den and catch him in action.'

So I got Mum to hang out some more washing and we sat and waited.

We waited a long time. Mum even brought us some dinner as we didn't want to come in to the house in case we missed him.

Nothing happened, except that Stacey came round and started interfering and trying to find out what we were doing, AGAIN.

MAYBE STACEY HAS
SOMETHING TO DO WITH THIS.

SATURDAY

Everything is going wrong and it has to be because I've lost my lucky underpants, I'm sure of it. I was at football camp today and played so badly: tripped over my own shoe laces, got nutmegged a million times, gave away a penalty and even scored an own goal. Everybody hated me and I think even James was pretending he'd never met me before. It was so embarrassing. If I don't find those pants soon, I don't know what I'll do.

To make matters worse, last night SOME MORE WASHING WENT MISSING. This time it was my dad's T-shirt and Mum was not happy. She said she's not going to put any more washing on the line until we've found out who the thief is. If only we'd waited a bit longer and if only stupid Stacey hadn't interfered, then we might have caught the thief in action.

Stacey is in our class at school. She's bossy and annoying. Me and James pull her hair (him more than me) and call her a cry-baby and she's always telling the teacher on us. She doesn't like us and we don't like her. But she still comes into my garden bugging us all the time. I don't get it.

We think Stacey might have taken the washing after we'd left, so we've been spying on her today, which isn't easy as she always seems to catch us. First, we sneaked into her garden and had a search in her playhouse for evidence. There were a few things that looked as if they could be stolen washing, like a table cover, a tea towel and an old coat and dress. We didn't find any of the missing things though.

Then we hid in the bushes with Dad's video camera and waited for Stacey and her friend to come into the garden. Unfortunately, we left her back gate open and Brosnan came sniffing around and found us. Stacey went screaming indoors. We ran off back to our lookout den, but about 10 minutes later my mum came down and gave us a long lecture about spying on girls. She took our binoculars and video camera off us. Stacey and her friend were there too. They looked so smug. I hate girls.

It also turns out that the things in the playhouse are old hand-me-downs, so Stacey probably isn't the thief either.

SUNDAY

Last night, the old football and the chewed-up trainer we found when we went hunting for clues the other day went missing. This is getting ridiculous.

James decided to sleep over tonight, as we were determined to crack this case. We knew it wasn't Stacey, Mrs O'Connor or Gruesome Newsome, but we still thought the thief was close by. We'd come this far, we were not going to give up that easily. That's why we decided to do another stake-out and we've only just finished. This is what happened:

I convinced Mum to do some more washing, so we could put it on the line to tempt the thief. She wasn't pleased, as there weren't many dirty clothes left. She said I would have to do all the ironing and so I agreed, hoping she'd forget she ever asked me. We warned Stacey not to come anywhere near us or we'd show everyone in school the video that shows her playing with dolls like a little girl. We got Max to take Brosnan for a walk so he'd be too tired to stay out with us (I had to pay him) and we took loads of snacks to the lookout den so we wouldn't have to keep going back to the house.

We didn't want to take any chances and scare the thief away this time.

At 8:00 p.m., something finally happened. The bushes between Mrs O'Connor's house and ours started rustling.

'Someone's coming,' I whispered to James. We sat still as statues.

'What can you see?' I asked, as James had the binoculars (we'd managed to convince Mum to give us those back when we explained what we needed them for).

'It's a fox,' said James.

'Oh, is that all?' I was disappointed, but I took the binoculars from James to see for myself anyway.

You would not believe what I saw.

The fox went up to our washing line, jumped up and pulled down one of my T-shirts with his teeth.

'The fox is the thief,' I said to James. 'Can you believe that? What would he want with all those clothes?'

We watched the fox go back into the thick hedge.

'That must be where he lives,' said James. 'Shall we sneak in and have a look?'

We peered into the hedge and stopped as we came face to face with the fox thief. I thought my heart had stopped beating as he stood there staring straight at us. Then we looked down and saw three cubs and realised it was actually a mother fox. You could just see Mrs O'Connor's underskirt and Stacey's T-shirt peeping out from under them. She had taken the clothes to use as a bed for her cubs.

We smiled at the fox and backed out of the hedge very slowly.

I didn't see my lucky underpants though. I think they've disappeared for good and the fox didn't take them after all. Perhaps it was someone else; someone who knew they were special pants. That person, or thing, might be running around in them right now (or flying, perhaps). They could be a superhero with the power to bring good luck. I wish I had them back. I don't feel as though I've been a good agent so far. James has beaten me to every meeting, he was the one who was brave enough to knock on Gruesome Newsome's mum's door and we seem to keep getting into trouble. There was no washing thief after all that either, just a silly fox who prefers clothes as a bed instead of leaves. What will happen if there is a real mystery to solve?

HOW AM I EVER GOING TO BE A SECRET AGENT IF I DON'T HAVE THOSE LUCKY PANTS TO HELP ME?

PART 2

Week 2
Becoming a Double Agent,
by James Murphy

.

SUNDAY

It was rubbish finding out that a fox stole the washing. I was hoping it was going to be a runaway prisoner who was stealing stuff so he could escape the country with a new identity. We hadn't heard of any escaped prisoners, so that was unlikely, but still, it would have been cool. We could have been on telly and everything and we might have even got a massive reward.

I've decided it might get a bit boring doing this secret agent thing if the only mysteries we find are to do with stolen washing. Anyway, this whole thing was Harry's idea and that's why he got to be Harry Bond. I mean, come on, my name is James, so it should have been me who got to have the 'Bond' bit. We couldn't think of any other famous secret agents, so I was just going to be Agent James, but my dad gave me the idea of being James Hunt, as in Ethan Hunt from *Mission Impossible*, so I went with that.

Now I've come up with my own way to make this secret agency more fun. We're going to become double agents. This means that as well as solving mysteries (if there are any more) we are going to play tricks on people.

Starting with Stacey. Let's face it, she's annoying anyway AND she's a girl.

I have a box of tricks and joke stuff that my granddad bought me for Christmas. It's time to put it to good use.

Can't wait!

MONDAY

Today was awesome. I have been at Harry's as usual, starting with a meeting in the agency headquarters, where I told him all about my plan to play tricks on people. I reckon he was a bit miffed he didn't come up with the idea himself, but he thought my plan to get Stacey first was so cool.

The best thing was my cat, Jasper, brought a mouse in last night. When Mum went downstairs this morning, she screamed and then shouted at me to come help her. When I saw the mouse, with its head bitten off and its guts hanging out, I just knew it would be perfect for what I had in mind. I put it in an old shoebox and took it outside, pretending to Mum I had put it in the bin.

By the time I got to Harry's house, the mouse was starting to smell a bit, so it was even more perfect. The first thing we did was to sneak into Stacey's back garden and put the mouse in the pretend saucepan on the top of the play cooker. At school Stacey always tries to make out that she is really grown up and mature, but we know she still plays with that stuff when she's at home, especially when she plays with her little sister, who isn't quite as annoying as Stacey is.

We set up all the tricks, then went and knocked on the door. Stacey answered.

'What do you want?' Stacey asked.

'Do you want to come and join our club?' I asked.

'What, me?' she said, pulling a face that suggested she didn't really believe us, so I nudged Harry in the ribs, then quickly hid my hands behind my back (I didn't want her to see what was on them).

'Yeah, well, we thought we could do with more people and you'd do,' Harry said. I rolled my eyes at him and shook my head.

'Look, Stacey, do you want to come or what?' I said.

'Yeah, OK then,' Stacey said, jumping off the steps and skipping down the garden in her annoying girly way.

We ran ahead of her to get back to the den first and when we were all inside I initiated trick number 1.

'Here, Stacey, have a sweet,' I said.

'What's this for?' she said, as she unwrapped it and popped it into her mouth.

'Peace offering for the other day,' said Harry. 'You know, the filming and stuff.'

Stacey seemed embarrassed.

'Oh, that… well, it's nothing,' she said. 'So what's the club all about then?'

'We can't tell you until you've completed the initiation process,' I said. (Trick number 2.)

'How do I do that?'

'Well, it's more of a ceremony,' I said, and got us to stand in a circle in the middle of the room.

'We have to each put a thumb on the other person's forehead like this,' I said. So they both copied me. 'Then we say the words: "I promise to do my utmost to solve any mysteries that come my way."'

I was trying so hard not to laugh I almost wet myself.

'Then you have to turn around in a circle like this,' I said, demonstrating, 'and put your thumbs back onto each other's foreheads again. Then we say: "I promise to keep everything that happens in these four walls a secret, on fear of death."'

We all chanted the words then Stacey screamed.

'What's wrong?' I said.

'There is an enormous spider on that bench over there,' she said, backing away. (Trick number 3.)

'Oh that,' said Harry. 'We get them all the time in here. Don't worry about it, Stacey, you get used to it. Here, why don't you sit down on this chair?'

Stacey sat down and there came the most enormous fart noise (trick number 4). Harry and I laughed so hard we fell on the floor. Then Stacey stood up, holding a whoopee cushion in her hands.

'This was all a big joke, wasn't it? I hate you two,' she said, throwing down the whoopee cushion and running out of the den.

We got up off the floor and ran through Stacey's gate after her, sneaking up to hide in the bush near to her house. We could hear her mum talking.

'Stacey, what have you done to your face, there are black marks all over it?'

'What do you mean, Mum?'

'Urgh, and why is your mouth all blue?'

29

'Argh, Harry and James, I'm going to kill you!' Stacey screamed.

We legged it back to Harry's house and stayed indoors for a while, hoping Stacey would calm down and wouldn't come after us.

Later, when we were back in the lookout den with Brosnan, we heard a scream from next door. We ran out to the back gate in time to see Stacey and her sister running up the garden back to their house.

'There's a dead mouse in the saucepan,' Stacey screamed. 'And I bet I know who put it there.'

We ran back to our den again and this time we barred the door.

'That was really fun,' said Harry. 'But I don't know if it will stop her from interfering in our business or just make it worse.'

'Who cares?' I said. 'It was worth it to see her face. Did you see all those black ink marks from our thumbs and her mouth all blue from the sweet? It was so funny. I can't wait to tell the others at school.'

'So who's next then?' Harry asked.

We both agreed it had to be Gruesome Newsome. So we made a plan for the next day.

TUESDAY

We decided not to do too many jokes on Gruesome Newsome in case he had a heart attack and died or something; then we might end up getting done by the police. So we put some fake dog poo on his front doorstep and let off a stink bomb. I knocked on his door and we ran away and hid across the street behind a car.

When he came out and caught the smell, then saw the poo, Gruesome Newsome swore so much and so loudly, we couldn't believe it. Now we know he's not as posh as he makes out. I hope the stink bomb smell went into his house and stayed there for ages.

Next, we hid fake tissue money in various places all over the streets (ours and the next two along) and watched as people picked them up thinking they'd found a real-life fifty-pound note. The expression on their faces when they realised the money wasn't real was hilarious. Then they would look around the street suspiciously as if someone from the telly was going to jump out in front of them and shout 'got you'. Harry and I decided we should make a TV programme like this when we're older.

'What shall we do now?' Harry said. 'This is getting a bit old.'

He's so boring sometimes.

'No, it's not, we've only just started,' I said. 'We've still got the sneezing powder and the severed thumb yet.'

Harry groaned.

'Aw, come on,' I said. 'I know, let's go back to mine. I've got an idea.'

Back at my house, we checked to see if my sister was around. Kate is twelve but thinks she's a teenager. As luck would have it, she was with her best friend, Chloe, who happens to be scared of everything.

After we'd made sure Kate and Chloe were outside and could see us, Harry and I went to the bottom of the garden to climb the tree. I pretended to fall and Harry started shouting, 'Argh, James, what's happened to your thumb?'

I was crying out in pretend pain. 'I don't know but it hurts.'

'Oh no, I think your thumb has come off,' Harry said, but he's really not that good at acting, so I was worried it wouldn't work.

'Kate, help,' I cried. 'Quick, Harry, pick it up and go get some ice.'

Harry took the thumb and wrapped it in a hankie.

'What have you got there?' Kate said, as she came over with Chloe.

'James' thumb fell off when he was climbing the tree. Here, do you want to see?' Harry thrust the thumb right into Chloe's face.

'Oh my God, ARGH!' she screamed and ran off.

'Don't just stand there with it, you idiot,' Kate shouted, 'go get some ice, get Mum, QUICK. James, are you OK? I can't believe this is happening.'

Chloe was still screaming in the background. Kate was hysterical and almost crying. Then she stopped in her tracks.

'Why are you laughing?'

Harry was clutching his stomach and I was lying on the ground with tears pouring out of my eyes – tears of laughter, of course.

'Why you little…'

Harry and I bolted out of the back gate with Kate chasing after us. We were much faster than her and as we legged it we could hear her shouting, 'You horrible, disgusting pigs! I'm going to tell Mum on you.'

She is such a tell-tale, even though she is twelve.

We ran all the way to the park before we stopped and collapsed, from laughter and from all the running.

'OK, you win, that was so worth it,' Harry said.

'Yeah, I know, but I have a feeling we won't be able to get away with any more tricks tomorrow,' I said. 'We'll have to think of something else to do.'

WEDNESDAY

What did I tell you? No more tricks. When we eventually decided to leave the park, thinking it would be safe to go home, we went to Harry's house only to be greeted by his mum, who was very cross because Gruesome Newsome had lectured her for about an hour.

'He saw you running away from his house after you knocked on the door, Harry, so he knows it was you two who left the poo and stink bomb.'

Both of us chuckled when she said 'poo'. I don't know why, it just sounded funny.

'Don't laugh, I'm being serious. How do you think I felt having him come round here telling me I don't know how to bring up my own children?'

Fair comment, I suppose. Who would like a lecture from Gruesome Newsome? Not me, that's for sure. We got up to leave.

'Don't move, I haven't finished yet,' Harry's mum said.

So we sat straight back down in our chairs, groaning. We both knew what was coming next.

'I've had Stacey's mum round here as well.'

Yep, just as we thought.

'What you did to her today was just plain old mean. If you don't want to play with her then just ignore her or leave her be. There was no need to play those tricks. I'm disappointed in you both.'

We both hung our heads, pretending to be ashamed of what we had done. Well, I did anyway, but Harry was doing a good impression of actually looking really upset, and he's a rubbish actor.

'Tomorrow you are both going to apologise to Stacey and Mr Newsome and then you are spending the day apart.'

We started to moan in protest, but Mrs Smith raised her hand in the air and stopped us.

'Don't start that, I have spoken to your mum, James, and she agrees with me, so it's done.'

We moaned about how unfair it all was and Harry stomped off to his room. I left and went home, where I got the same lecture from my mum.

'Blah, blah, blah,' I said as she went on at me. I was sent to my room for the rest of the evening.

So that was what happened at the end of yesterday, and that pretty much explains what we have been doing today: no secret agency, no double agents, just boring apologising and then sitting at home, at the desk in the study. The only thing to look at from there is the embarrassing old photos on the wall of us when we were babies and the view out of the back of the house, which is the bit where we put the bins. Mum made me do homework that's not even due until September. Kate and Chloe laughed at me, so I stuck two fingers up at them. But Mum saw and I got into even more trouble.

This holiday is not turning out well. Luckily, I'm allowed to play with Harry again tomorrow but we've been told if we get into any more trouble we won't be allowed to play together for the rest of the holidays. Where is the fun in that?

Annoyed!

News flash: there may have been a development. I've just been out in the back garden practising some penalties and noticed there was a light coming from the house at the end of the road.

'Mum, why is there a light on in the old haunted house?' I asked when I went back inside.

'Do you mean number 35? Oh, well you would have missed all that today, wouldn't you?'

'Missed all what?' I said. I hate it when she goes all cryptic on me.

'Someone moved in there,' Mum said. 'Though Lord knows why anyone would want to move into that old place.'

'Someone? Who – did you see them?' I asked. I was cross I hadn't been around to watch the removals van and all the stuff being taken into the house.

'Well that's just it – no one seems to know who it is. It's a bit of a mystery really.'

Maybe we have just found our second case.

THURSDAY

Today we sat outside number 35 waiting to see who had moved in, but we didn't see anyone. It was weird hanging around that horrible old house because it's different to all the others on our street. Mum said it was here before all the others were built, when it was a farm instead of a road. The house has a big black gate and a massive front garden and you can hardly see the house through all the trees and bushes. It's one of those houses that no one seems to live in for very long, which is why we think it's haunted.

No one has lived in number 35 for ages and we haven't been near it since last summer when we played dares with Tom and Luke from school. Harry dared them to go and sit in the back garden for five minutes and after about a minute they both came screaming out of the drive, saying they saw the shadow of someone inside. I didn't know whether to believe them but to be on the safe side I've kept away from there.

Today, the house seemed even more haunted than ever, the stone it's built from darker coloured and the paint around the windows with more cracks. Perhaps it's because we'd never looked at it so closely and for so long before. All the windows had old curtains in them, some of them drawn shut and others left open or hanging off. There must be a big gap in one of the upstairs windows, because the curtains in there were blowing in the breeze. It made the hairs on the back of my neck and arms stand up. I didn't tell Harry that though.

Harry thought we should stay on the other side of the road to get a better view of who was coming and going. I agreed, but we had to sit on the pavement in front of number 26 for ages and it got a bit uncomfortable, not to mention boring. That was when I came up with a really good idea to pass the time.

'Why don't we make up our own language so we can talk in code?'

'Awesome,' Harry said.

The first idea I came up with was to swap the first and last letters of every word to make a new one. So if I wanted to say, 'Hello, I'm Agent James Hunt,' I would actually say:

'Oellh, M'I tgenta Samej Tunh.'

This was quite hard and took lots of practice. Ew tas eutsido rumben 35 lla yad tub ehert saw gothinn ot treporr. Ohw sah dovem ni ot rumben 35?

The problem was Harry is so bad at spelling I couldn't work out what he was trying to say, so we had to give up on that one. There's no point in having a secret code if you can't even understand it yourself, is there?

The next idea was Harry's. He said we should say every word backwards. That was quite fun until Alex from number 26 came out to see what we were doing. We were sitting in front of his house after all.

'Why are you talking backwards?' he said to us.

'How did you know that?' I said. 'We were talking in a secret code.'

'It's hardly secret, is it?' he said. 'Everyone does that.'

Alex is in the year below us at school, so we knew we would have to come up with something else.

Our third and final idea was the one we decided to go with. If there is an 'a, e, i, o or u' in the word we had to change it to 'iz'.

So, 'I am James Hunt' would be: 'Iz izm Jizmcs Hiznt.'

Harry Bond is 'Hizrry Biznd.'

That made sitting watching an empty house so much more fun and when we eventually decided to call it a day (which was only because we were so hungry), we went back to my house and practised in front of my mum and Kate and Chloe. Mum just tutted and shook her head but Kate and Chloe got annoyed because they didn't know what we were saying about them or why we were laughing. That meant our secret language code actually worked.

We also went to Harry's house to try it out there. Unfortunately, it didn't work on his big brother. Instead, he hung Harry upside down by his ankles and threatened to drop him on his head if he didn't stop. We gave up after that.

We may be secret double agents, with our own language, but we have no idea what is going on in number 35. Today there was no one there again. We even went up the drive and looked around. Well, Harry did. We flipped a coin to see who would do it and he lost. He muttered something about that being typical bad luck for him because he lost his lucky underpants. I wish he would stop going on about them, it's getting boring.

Harry said there was furniture and stuff in the house, so it looked like someone had moved in, but where are they?

We did find one lead though. There was the old 'for let' sign in the front garden with the name of the estate agents, so we went there to see if we could find out the names of the new people from them.

Happy Moves Estate Agency seemed surprised when we walked in.

'How can we help you young men?' a lady sitting at the front desk said. It was then we both looked at each other and realised we hadn't thought about what we were going to say. Harry shrugged his shoulders and went bright red. He just looked at me instead. He always makes me do the asking.

'Erm, we have come to ask about a house on Trinity Grove,' I said.

'Why, are you interested in buying it?' she said, and I could tell she was trying not to laugh. I felt a bit silly but carried on anyway.

'It's number 35, do you know if it's still on the market?' I asked.

The lady checked her computer and told us that it had been let already, which we kind of knew anyway.

'Oh, could you tell us who to, please?' I asked.

'I'm afraid I'm not allowed to tell you that, young man,' she said. I hate it when people call me 'young man'.

'OK then, thanks,' I said, and dragged Harry out of the door.

'Was that it?' Harry said when we got outside. 'You didn't expect them to just come right out and say who it was did you?'

'Well, I didn't see you coming up with a better idea,' I said, annoyed he was having a go at me. 'You do the talking next time,' I said. 'Izm gizizng hizme.' And then I left him there.

I'm a bit fed up of this secret agency. It's not been any fun since we did the double agent days. Anyway, I'm at football camp this weekend, so I won't be able to work on the case again until next week. That is, if there is any case to work on.

Man of the match, top goal scorer and a definite place in the pre-season cup match team, I'm sure. That's how well football camp went today. It's a shame I can't say the same thing about Harry. He played so badly again, just like last week. I don't know what's got in to him lately. He's normally a good player, one of our best defenders, though I would never tell him that to his face. It seems like he's forgotten how to play altogether.

All the team kept having a go at Harry today and I felt sorry for him. I could see the coaches shaking their heads too, as well as some of the mums and dads who were watching, and that's never a good thing. Harry looked miserable and I asked him what was going on after the match.

'It's because I haven't got my lucky pants anymore,' he said. 'I used to play so well when I had them and now I've lost them I'm useless.'

'You can't blame losing some dumb old pants for the way you play football,' I told him. 'You've got to get over it, they're gone and they won't stop you playing football or doing anything else.'

Harry looked hurt as he turned and walked away from me. I felt bad for talking to him like that. It's the truth though. Harry knows I don't believe in stuff like that and he needs to realise he can play football just fine, with or without Spiderman pants on. I hope he gets it together before the coaches choose the team for the next game. If he's left out of the squad, he will be gutted and so will I. It won't be the same playing without him.

PART 3

Week 3
Secret Diary of Stacey Webster

It's not fair. There are no girls my age on this street. I have to live next to horrible Harry Smith instead and he plays all the time with James Murphy, who is really mean to me. That's what I will call them from now on, Horrible Harry and Meany Murphy.

I hate boys. They are disgusting and they stink because they never wash properly. I don't even think Harry ever brushes his hair – those curls of his make him look just like his dog – as for James, well he thinks he's a Premiership footballer or something, with that stupid long bit of hair he styles on the top of his head. Urgh, I can't even think about them.

The school holiday is soooo boring because all my friends have gone away and we are the only ones who aren't having a holiday. Mum said we couldn't afford it because they have spent all their money doing work on the house. Dad has to work, like all the time until midnight every day or something, and Mum has also got a job doing cleaning, so every day we are stuck at home with Granny looking after us.

Most of the other kids on our street are either boys

or loads older than me. The only person I have to play with is my sister, Kim. She's OK but she's only six and all she ever wants to play is mummies and babies.

I wanted to join the secret agency that Horrible Harry and Meany Murphy made up because it sounded cool. I was going to be like Carmen Cortez from *Spy Kids*: Agent Stacey Cortez. But then they did horrible things and spoiled it all. I know I fell for their stupid tricks but if they think they're getting away with it then they are SO WRONG.

There was no one in the shed at the bottom of Horrible Harry's garden today (that's the place where they have their stupid meetings). I knocked on Harry's door just to make sure and his mum said they were both up at Meany Murphy's house. Well, she didn't say 'Meany Murphy's'; she just said 'James' house' but you know what I mean. Anyway, that was good news for me. With both of them out of the way, it gave me an idea and you would not believe what I did. I went into their stupid den and found their box of tricks. I wasn't sure which one to use but then I saw the sneezing powder and I had the idea to sprinkle it all over the place, so the next time they go in there they will be sneezing their heads off. I'm going to set up my own secret club and I will get back at them for what they did to me. My first task is to spy on the boys to find out what goes on in this secret agency of theirs.

As predicted, because they are so boring and predictable, Meany Murphy came round to Horrible Harry's this morning and they went to their den. I know this because I was hiding out in the playhouse at the bottom of my garden, which is my own mission control room, and when I heard them come down the path in Horrible Harry's garden I got myself into position, which was right by the fence on my side.

I had the small stepladder from the garage and the hosepipe and I was all ready for action. It wasn't long before I heard the sneezing start and after about twenty sneezes the door flung open and Horrible Harry and Meany Murphy came rushing out. I know all this because there is a spy hole in the middle of the fence.

Both of them were sneezing and rubbing their eyes and had tears streaming down their faces. That was my cue. I stood up on the stepladder so I could see over the fence.

'Oh, what's the matter with you two?' I said. 'Got hay fever or something?'

'We can't… atchoo… stop… atchoo… sneezing…

49

atchoo,' said Horrible Harry. 'My throat… atchoo… hurts.'

'I wonder what could have caused that?' I said. 'You need some water. Would you like me to get you some?'

'Yes… atchoo… please… atchoo,' said Meany Murphy.

'OK then,' I said. 'Here you go.'

And I turned on the hosepipe and aimed it straight at them.

'You said you wanted water, didn't you?' I shouted.

Horrible Harry and Meany Murphy both stood there screaming like babies as I soaked them through. They tried to run away but I kept aiming it at them. Eventually they ran further up the garden and I couldn't reach them anymore.

Two tricks in one and they hadn't even suspected a thing. Ha. I turned off the hose and sat down on the stepladder. I was feeling really pleased with myself until…

I was suddenly soaked from above. I screamed and jumped off the ladder. They had gone and got their own hosepipe and were aiming it at me from over their side of the garden. IT WAS WAR.

I turned the hosepipe on again and aimed it back. It was like we were having a shoot-out, except we were using hosepipes instead of guns. The top of our hose is a bit like a gun and you can make the water come out of it by squeezing the handle like a trigger. Horrible Harry has one just the same. So I was squatting on the top of my ladder, sneaking a look to see where my enemies were (they were hiding in the bushes) and whenever one of them peeped out I would aim at them. Then I had to duck back down so I didn't get hit.

Before long we were all soaked and laughing our heads off. In the end Horrible Harry was even squirting Meany Murphy and by the time we'd finished none of us was hiding anymore, we were just squirting each other and getting more and more soaked (if that's possible).

The only reason we stopped was because Horrible Harry's mum said we had to turn the water off as we were wasting it and if we didn't then there'd end up being a hosepipe ban altogether.

'Truce,' Meany Murphy said.

'OK, then,' I agreed.

'That was the best fun I've had all holiday so far,' Horrible Harry said.

And for once all three of us actually agreed on something.

'Did you put sneezing powder in our den?' Horrible Harry said.

'Erm, yes,' I said, 'but that was to get you back for what you did the other day.'

'I think we're even now, then,' Meany Murphy said.

And we all agreed again – UNBELIEVABLE.

I had to go in and get changed after that. Maybe Horrible Harry and Meany Murphy aren't so horrible and mean after all and I can stop calling them that. And at least they won't smell so bad now that they have had a good wash.

WEDNESDAY

Today I spied on Harry and James (see, I'm being nice now) when they were having a meeting in their den. I heard them discussing the old house at the end of our road, the one everyone is talking about because some new neighbours have moved in, but no one has seen them. Harry and James are trying to find out who they are, but they haven't seen anyone going in or coming out of the house either.

I also heard James say he thought I wasn't so bad after all – even though I am a girl. What is that supposed to mean? They are stupid boys and girls are much better and smarter. If they can't find out who is living in number 35 I bet I can.

It was easy actually. I asked my granny and she knows everything. Well, she knows Mrs O'Connor and she definitely knows everything.

'Granny,' I said. 'Do you know who has moved into number 35?'

'I was talking to Mrs O'Connor about it just yesterday,' Granny said (I told you Mrs O'Connor knows everything). 'She watched the removals van and there were only the removals people going in and out, no one else was anywhere to be seen. Then she took one of her special Victoria sponge cakes round there and no one answered the door, so she left a note to say who it was from.'

'Did they eat it?' I asked.

'Well they left the tin and a note outside her door the next day,' Granny said. 'It said "thank you for the lovely cake, from Barry and Shona."'

Barry and Shona – see, I've got names already.

'But she still hasn't seen them?'

'No, but the interesting thing is, she has noticed a car coming and going every night.'

So tonight, I have stayed up really late. My mum doesn't know and she'd be so cross if she found out I was still awake at 10:00 p.m. I am writing this using my torch, whilst hiding under my duvet so I won't get found out.

I've seen the car coming to number 35. There is a good view of the house from my bedroom window, which is at the front. I saw Barry and Shona in the car because the street lights are right outside my house. What was really weird is that they were both wearing sunglasses, in the dark!

The car went up the drive and Barry and Shona got out and went into the house. An hour later, they came out, got in the car again and drove off.

I don't know where Barry and Shona are in the daytime or why they only come to their house at night, but I think I have enough evidence now to go to Harry and James with. If they want to know what I know then they'll have to let me join their club, won't they?

This morning I went to Harry's back garden at exactly 9:00 a.m. because I knew they would be having their meeting. When I knocked on the door and James answered, he seemed really surprised.

'What are you doing here? No girls allowed,' he said. I ignored him.

'I have some information about the new people in number 35,' I said. 'If you want to know what it is, you will have to let me be a secret agent too.'

James stared at me for a moment, then said (in a kind of fake posh voice), 'I will discuss this with my partner and get back to you shortly.'

Then he shut the door in my face and left me standing there.

About twenty hours later (well, it felt like that) Harry opened the door and peeped out. I don't know why he had to do that; it's not as though I don't know what it looks like inside the den.

'My fellow agent and I have discussed your application to join the agency and we have decided that we are prepared to give you a trial of one day,' he said, also in a silly posh voice. What was wrong with them today?

I rolled my eyes at him

'I want to be in for the whole of this case,' I said. 'That or nothing. You are not having my information then solving the mystery without me.'

Then he shut the door on me AGAIN. And I stood and waited for another twenty hours AGAIN. Finally, the door opened and both Harry and James came out this time.

'Deal,' they said together.

I wanted to do a victory punch in the air and shout 'yes' but I kept it to myself because I didn't want them to know how happy I was about being able to join their gang. So instead I said very calmly, 'Shall we continue the meeting, so that I can brief you with my findings?'

This time it was my turn to talk in a strange voice. It was obviously catching.

During the meeting, I told Harry and James about Barry and Shona and the strange comings and goings in the night.

'There's definitely no one there in the daytime,' said James. 'We've already done a stake out and we even sneaked up to the house. There was no one around.'

'No, actually, I was the one who looked around,' said Harry. 'And I swear I saw a shadow.'

'You were just spooked because we think it's haunted,' said James.

'OK,' I said, interrupting them. 'Maybe there is much more to this than meets the eye. There could be something ghostly going on, but do you want to know what I think?' I stared at them both, waiting for them to nod at me. 'I think they could be vampires.'

'Vampires,' they both said at once.

'Think about it – up at night, nowhere to be seen during the day, wearing dark glasses, it all makes perfect sense.'

Well, it did to me anyway.

I could tell by their faces both Harry and James were thinking it through. So I waited, patiently, for them to come round to the idea.

'Perhaps she's right,' Harry said to James. James nodded at him. I smiled, pleased they had listened to my idea.

'What do we do about it then?' James said.

We made a plan.

 Today I went to the meeting in Harry's den at 9:00 a.m. again. When I walked in, it stank.

'Urgh, what's that smell?' I said.

'It's Harry,' said James. 'He reeks of garlic.'

'Yeah, I got Mum to make a spaghetti bolognese and I put loads of extra garlic in it when she wasn't watching,' he said, looking pleased with himself.

James and I glanced at each other.

'Harry, you are not supposed to eat the garlic to repel the vampires; you are supposed to wear it round your neck.' I said.

'Yeah, you're such an idiot,' said James. 'But you don't have to worry, no one will come anywhere near you because you smell so bad.'

Then Harry punched him.

'OK, you two, what else did you bring?' I asked. 'I brought this cross.'

'I brought this stake,' James said. 'You know, a stake through the heart – isn't that right?'

'Yeah, but that's not a stake, it's a wooden play knife,' I said. 'It's not even sharp.'

'Well, maybe vampires have thin skin,' James said.

'You better hope so, because otherwise we are going to be vampire dinner,' I said.

Harry seemed worried.

'You're not scared are you, Harry?' I said.

'No, I just don't think we have a plan,' he said. 'All we have are a few weapons to protect us against vampires – but how are we going to find out if that's what they really are?'

'We need to keep these weapons just in case, so when we do meet them we are protected.'

'What do you mean "when"?' Harry said.

'We're going to hide out in their garden tonight and watch what they do when they come to the house,' I said, folding my arms across my chest. I thought I saw James nodding his head in approval, but he seemed to quickly turn away from me when he realised I was looking at him.

'I won't be allowed out at night,' Harry said.

'Who cares if we're allowed or not?' I said. 'Our parents won't know we're out because we won't tell them, silly. Do you think mine would let me out at night either? Course not. We have to sneak out.'

'I'm not sure I like the sound of this,' said Harry.

'Do you want to find out what Shona and Barry are up to or not?' I said. 'We won't find anything by sitting outside their house all day. This a secret agency, right? I thought you were spies and this is what spies do.'

Harry and James seemed to communicate just by

staring at each other. I folded my arms and tapped one of my feet on the floor to show them my impatience.

'I think she's right,' said James, without looking at me. 'We've got to do this.'

Harry nodded slowly.

'Great,' I said. 'We'll rendezvous back at the den at twenty-one hundred hours.'

I jumped up feeling excited. 'Ha, I've always wanted to say "rendezvous". This is so cool, I can't wait. See you later, spy friends.'

SATURDAY

I am in my room because I'm grounded. It's where I've been all day and it's so not fair because it's Saturday and I was supposed to go to London Zoo with Annabel (who is my BFF, by the way), but Mum said after what I did last night I'd be lucky if I ever left the house again. No way am I staying in this house forever.

As I've nothing better to do, I might as well tell you what happened. I pretended to go to bed at the normal time but instead got dressed and waited until it was nearly 9:00 p.m. Then I crept downstairs and tiptoed straight past the lounge where Mum and Dad were watching the telly and out the back door into the garden. It was easy.

I was the first one at the den. James came next, then Harry, who looked like he had already been asleep. His hair was all messy and he was still in his pyjamas.

'You really don't look like a secret agent dressed like that,' I said.

'Shut up, Stacey, or I won't let you be in the agency anymore,' he said.

'Can't do that, you made a promise.'

'Don't care.'

'Don't care,' I mimicked back.

'Pack it in, you two, we've got a job to do, remember,' James said.

We had agreed to sneak in through the front gate of number 35 and hide somewhere in the garden. When we got there, we found a spot that was large enough for us all to squeeze in together, in between a broken old greenhouse and a big barrel. It felt like we waited a really long time and I'm sure Harry fell asleep. He was snoring and when his head fell on my shoulder I nudged him in the ribs, which made him jump. Just then, a light came on in the house.

'I think they're here,' I whispered.

We couldn't see much from where we were hiding so I made a suggestion.

'Let's spread out and get a closer look,' I said.

'Who said you could be leader of this agency?' said Harry. 'Since you joined all you've done is boss us about.'

'I'm not, but I got the information and this was my plan, that's all. And anyway, you two are rubbish. You didn't find anything out.'

'Yes, we did, we found out lots of things, we just didn't tell YOU.'

That was when we realised we were both standing up, facing each other, almost nose to nose and shouting.

'Excuse me, what do you think you are doing in my garden at this time of night?'

When we heard the voice, Harry and I both froze.

'This is your fault,' Harry said, poking me in the chest.

'No it's not, you started it,' I snapped back.

'No you started it.'

'Liar.'

'Liar.'

'When you've quite finished, would one of you like to explain what this is all about?'

I looked at Harry and we both turned to face the man, who we presumed was Barry. I clutched my cross really tightly and hoped that Harry's garlic breath would be bad enough to save us both.

'Erm, we lost our ball in your garden and came in to look for it but couldn't find it and then we were just trying to work out who threw it in here. Harry said I threw it in but I didn't, so...'

'What are you doing out at this time at night? You should be in bed. Do your parents know you're out?'

'Yes,' I said.

'No,' Harry said, so I nudged him in the ribs.

'Idiot.'

'Well, we'd better go find out which one of you is telling the truth then, hadn't we?' Barry (we thought) said. He took us both by the arm and started to drag us out of the garden. I looked all around for James but couldn't see him anywhere.

'Don't be worrying about your ball,' said Barry, 'Whatever lands on my property becomes my property, and I don't want to ever see either of you in here again or you will become my property as well. Do you understand?'

I nodded.

'Please don't eat us,' Harry said.

'What are you talking about?' said Barry. 'Blooming kids.'

So after making us tell him where we lived, Barry marched us over to Harry's house first, where he explained to Mrs Smith that he had found us in his garden and could she please make sure her child does not escape the house in future? He also said would she kindly ensure her son does not trespass on his property ever again or the next time he would not be so understanding, and he said all of this without letting Harry's mum get a word in. Mrs Smith looked so shocked, all she could do was nod.

At my house, it was the same thing, but as soon as Barry left Mum and Dad went ballistic.

'What are you doing sneaking out of the house at this time of night?'

'Why were you in the garden at number 35?'

'You've no idea who that man is; don't you know anything about stranger danger?'

They weren't questions I was actually allowed to answer. I tried, but every time I went to open my mouth, a hand would rise in the air to stop me. The questions came at me one after the other until it seemed Mum and Dad had run out of things to say. They looked at each other and then they looked at me.

'At least you know who Barry from number 35 is now, eh?' I said.

That was when I was grounded and sent to my room.

SUNDAY

I haven't been allowed to go to Harry's today and Harry isn't allowed to come here either, but James came round as he didn't get caught last night. I was in my back garden when I heard a funny noise coming from the other side of the gate. When I went to get a better look I realised it was a 'psst' noise and that James was there. I stared at him through the gaps in the wooden panels.

'Don't tell anyone you've seen me,' he said, looking around as if to double check he was alone. He lowered his voice even more. 'Harry isn't allowed to have me round to play today so we're going to have to communicate in secret.'

'What are you doing, Stacey?' My little sister came skipping over when she realised I wasn't playing with her anymore.

'Oh, nothing, Kim, just picking some nice flowers for the playhouse,' I said, grabbing a few dandelions that were right by my feet. A piece of paper came sliding through the wood panels and I realised it was James poking it through. I grabbed it, stuffed it into my shorts, then went back to playing with Kim.

'Kimmy, I think we need fresh water to make some more tea,' I said. 'Do you want to go and get some?'

'OK,' she said, skipping off with the plastic teapot. When she left, I read the note. It said:

> *Sorry about last night. No point all of us being caught. Saw the suspects without their sunglasses on. No red eyes detected. Aren't vampires supposed to have red eyes? If you have any info, write it on the note then put it through the gate. I will pass it on to Harry.*
>
> *Agent James Hunt.*
> *Over and out.*

I rummaged around in an old plastic box full of junk and found a pencil. I wrote back:

> *No red eyes? Vampires definitely have red eyes. They didn't seem to notice the cross or Harry's breath either. Not sure they are vampires after all.*
>
> *Agent Cortez.*

This went on for the rest of the afternoon. We were trying to work out what Barry and Shona could be up to if they weren't vampires and why they only came to their house at night. We wondered if they had busy jobs and that's the only time they got to come back to their house. Then we thought maybe they were spies and the house is their meeting place. They could of course be criminals on the run and the house is their hideout. That was James' idea. He also thought Barry and Shona were burglars who spent all day robbing people's houses before returning to number 35 at night to hide their stash. That boy has a big imagination.

Eventually Brosnan started barking at the gate and, when he wouldn't stop, Harry's mum came down to see what was going on. James had to run away. I heard Harry telling his mum that Brosnan had been trying to catch a squirrel.

Tomorrow I can go round to Harry's again so we won't have to keep doing this. Yay. We need to work on a new plan to find out exactly what Barry and Shona are up to. I don't think waiting for them at night-time is a good idea any more, but we know for sure they are never there during the day, so we are going to have to investigate if we can get into their house somehow, or at least see in it. Harry won't like that, as he's a scaredy-cat, but he will have to stop being a baby or we'll never, ever find out what is going on and then we'll have to go back to school and it will be too late.

PART 4

Week 4
Secret Agent Diary by Harry Smith
(Agent Bond 009)

MONDAY

After the football camp disaster last week, I'm never playing football again. In fact, I don't think I will do any sports, or anything that means competing with James. Not without my lucky underpants, anyway.

No one seems to understand and every time I bring up the subject of where they might be, or ask Mum if they've turned up yet, I get either shouted at (by my brother) or told to give it a rest (by Mum).

Why don't they realise all this trouble I've been getting into is because I don't have those lucky pants anymore? I mean, getting caught hiding in Barry's garden and not getting anywhere with the mystery of number 35, having to let Stacey join the agency, it's all bad luck and bad luck happens when you don't have good luck anymore. It's like the law of physics, or something.

Talking of Stacey, she's taken over everything. AND she thinks she's so cool it makes me sick.

Stacey calls herself Agent Stacey Cortez, after one of the Spy Kids. It's stupid. I still don't like girls, but James said we had to let her join because we didn't have any more information and the only way we were going to be able to solve this mystery is with her help. I'm not so sure. I think we could have done it without her and the way he's carrying on you'd think he actually likes her.

Today we went round to see Mrs O'Connor because we thought she might know something about Barry and Shona. We kicked our football into her garden so we had an excuse to knock on her door and, as usual, she invited us in (which is what we were hoping for).

Mrs O'Connor always has really nice cakes and biscuits. She's always baking and has been testing it out on me and my brother for as long as I can remember. I LOVE Mrs O'Connor's baking. I wish my mum could make stuff like that but Mum doesn't do any baking at all; she just buys stuff from the supermarket, which is OK, I suppose, but not as good.

We arrived just as something was about to come out of the oven.

'Wow, what are you making today, Mrs O'Connor? Smells awesome,' I said.

'Come in, come in, you lovely lot, you're after my white choc chip cookies, so you are,' Mrs O'Connor said. That was actually what she said, the exact words. Mrs O'Connor talks Irish and it sometimes sounds funny.

'We came to get our football back, actually,' said James, 'but if you're offering…'

Mrs O'Connor shuffled to the kitchen to get the cookies out of the oven, and when James tried to grab one straight off the tray she smacked his hand away.

'Oi be off wit ya,' she said, 'Ye can't have it 'til it's cooled down a little.'

So we all sat at the table staring at the cookies, which were ENORMOUS, and the smell of them was making my stomach rumble and my mouth water.

'Would ya look at ye all,' said Mrs O'Connor, 'like little salivating puppies.'

I really had no idea what that meant, but Stacey sat there giggling.

'Mrs O, have you met the new neighbours yet?' James asked.

'I haven't but I hear ye two have,' she said looking at me and Stacey. I turned bright red and Stacey put her hand to her head and muttered 'so embarrassing.'

'We wanted to know why they only come to the house at night, that's all,' Stacey said.

'You're not the only one, lovey,' Mrs O'Connor said. 'I've been round there twice now. First with a Victoria sponge just after they moved in, then the other day I took round a tray of my finest tiffin, so I did, but there was no one there, so I left it on the doorstep with a note. Three days later I found the box on my doorstep with another note saying "thank you for the biscuits, they were lovely". I mean, "biscuits" – is that what they thought they were? They didn't even appreciate what I made for them or have the decency to knock on the door and thank me in person.'

We all sat there in silence, each of us looking disappointed.

'Mr Newsome has met them though.'

Suddenly we all sat up straight. GRUESOME NEWSOME HAS MET THE NEW NEIGHBOURS.

'Did he say anything about them? How did he meet

71

them? When?' We all asked questions at the same time.

'Calm down you's all. He met them when he was out walking his dog late the other night,' she said.

I didn't even know Gruesome Newsome had a dog.

'You see, he's quite an old dog, doesn't go out much but he needs his late-night walk so he doesn't do a pee pee in the night,' said Mrs O'Connor.

Stacey giggled and James did a funny cough thing.

'Did Grues…, I mean Mr Newsome say anything to you about them?' I said.

'Well, he said he was walking right by their house when they arrived on the drive and as they got out of their car Perky ran …'

James and Stacey burst out laughing.

'What?' said Mrs O'Connor, 'That's the name of his dog, so it is. Do you want to hear this or not?'

'Yes, yes, carry on Mrs O,' James said, trying to control his laughter. I shot him an irritated look, hoping he'd get the message.

'So, as I was saying, Perky ran off into their garden and grabbed something from Barry's hand. Mr Newsome said Perky isn't normally so naughty and he doesn't know what got into him but he wouldn't drop whatever it was. Barry, Shona and Mr Newsome ran round the garden after him and eventually Perky disappeared off and they couldn't find him. When he came back, whatever he'd run off with was nowhere to be seen. The man, Barry, was ever so cross and he told Mr Newsome if he ever let his dog on his property again he would have him put down. I don't think Mr Newsome was impressed.'

We all sat in silence again until James reached out his hand towards the cookies.

'They're cool now, look,' he said, picking one up.

'Go on, then, you can have one each and let me know what you think next time I see you. Be off with you now.'

We all sprinted towards the door and were just about to leave when Mrs O'Connor shouted from the kitchen.

'What about your football, boys? Don't forget to pick it up from the garden on your way out.'

'Oh, we don't need that right now,' I said, 'we've got loads more at home.'

And then we left.

THE QUESTION IS, WHAT DID PERKY TAKE FROM BARRY AND SHONA THAT WAS SO IMPORTANT – AND DID THEY FIND IT?

I couldn't sleep because I'm fed up of getting nowhere with this case. So I got up early and used Max's computer (because he stayed at a friend's house last night) to look up on the internet how to be a spy. I've been awake for ages and have found loads of cool stuff. I made a list of what we have to do. Here it is:

We need a leader or a captain and a deputy or vice-captain. I am going to say that I am the leader because this was my idea in the first place and we are using my shed for our meeting place. James can be the vice-captain and Stacey can be in charge of gadgets or something.

We need a base – check. This can be our secret meeting place as well as a place to rendezvous after a mission (that's when you meet up after).

We need to be able to communicate with each other and, as we don't have phones, the only thing we can use is walkie-talkies. I have some, which I forgot I even had, but we need another set so Stacey can have one too. Will have to discuss that in the meeting.

We also need binoculars (which we've got), secret camera (we will have to use the video camera and make do), gloves (so we don't leave fingerprints if we touch anything) and a mirror on a stick so we can see around corners.

We need to wear a disguise. I don't mean those silly glasses with funny noses and moustaches or anything, but perhaps we can use a hoody or Stacey could wear a wig or something. I've got sunshades and a baseball cap and I'm sure James has too.

We also need to make notes of everything – which is what I am doing in this secret agent diary. And we need to log everything we see, including times of Barry and Shona coming and going to the house.

We need to practise talking in different accents and use the code for talking and writing secret messages to each other so that no one will know what we are up to.

We need to gather intelligence for our mission – in other words, we need to know EXACTLY what the house is like, where each room is, make a map of the garden so we can find hiding places etc. and work out an escape route. Everyone needs to have a post, like a lookout station, at number 35.

Finally, we should all try to act naturally and make sure we cover our tracks. And it would be really good if we could also pick locks.

I'm going to take these notes to this morning's meeting so that we can formulate a proper plan. By the end of today we should have a map of Barry and Shona's garden and the outside of the house, so we'll know where all the doors and hiding places are. We might even try to get in. I don't think it's alarmed as it's so old and I haven't seen one of those box things on the front.

Hopefully, by the end of tomorrow we should have gathered some more intelligence and I'm hoping we will find some clues about what is happening there. I'm going to concentrate on this for now and try not to think about my lucky underpants and how bad my life is going to be without them.

The meeting went well, except the bit about who should be leader. James said it should be him because he is braver than me – so not true – and he didn't get caught by Barry the other day like Stacey and I did, so technically he is the best spy. I said I wouldn't have got caught if Stacey hadn't been there and it was his idea to let her in, so technically it was his fault I got caught. Stacey said she had contributed the most information to the mission so she should be the leader.

In the end, I won because I have all the equipment like the video camera and binoculars and walkie-talkies, and I said if the others wanted to use them AND use my den as a meeting place they would have to make me leader.

We went to see if we could get into the back garden of number 35 and found a hole in the fence just big enough for us to squeeze through. It's much better going in this way so no one asks why we are hanging around Barry and Shona's garden. We thought about putting on our disguises and walking straight in there, but with Mrs O'Connor, Gruesome Newsome and Stacey's granny always peeping out from behind their curtains, we knew we'd get recognised and told off again.

Whilst we were in the garden, we made a plan of it and found some really good hiding places. The hole in the fence is our getaway exit too, so that's another thing ticked off the list. Then we tried for ages to get into the house. There is no alarm (we checked), but we couldn't find a spare key even though we looked everywhere, under all the old plant pots and anywhere where it might be an obvious place to hide one. Barry and Shona are professionals.

James said he had read about picking locks and he'd brought some wire from his dad's garage with him. But he couldn't do it and in the end we had to give up. We spent the rest of our time looking around the garden trying to find the thing that Perky had taken from Barry. We were about to give up when …

'I've found something,' Stacey shouted.

'Sshhh,' James and I both said at the same time. Stupid Stacey might as well have let the whole street know what we were up to.

'Oops, sorry,' she whispered. 'But come here… look. Where are the gloves?'

Stacey put on the gloves I had brought and picked up something from the bushes.

'Urgh, it's all wet and sticky. Have you got an evidence bag?' she said.

'Here, I've got a sandwich bag,' said James.

We all looked at what Stacey was holding, wondering what it was.

'It looks like a passport to me,' James said.

When we got back to the den, we took exhibit number 1 (that's what we named it) out of the bag and examined it.

'It is a passport,' said Stacey. 'But this person doesn't look like either Barry or Shona.'

'So who is it then?' I said.

AND WHAT DID BARRY WANT WITH IT THAT WAS SO IMPORTANT?

We decided that whoever the passport belongs to must be important because of the way Barry and Shona reacted when Perky took it from them. That means we have something they want. Somehow, we have to lure them into a trap, pretending we are going to give it back (without telling them it's us, of course) and when we do, we can steal their keys and get into their house for a closer look.

I think the luring bit will be easy, as we can make a note by cutting out different letters from a newspaper and using them to make the words. I've seen that on the telly before. It's the trap bit we are stuck with. Here are our ideas so far:

We tell them a rendezvous point and, when they get there, we hide and we put the passport on top of a big pile of leaves covering a great big hole. When they try to get it, they will fall into the hole and be trapped. Only trouble is, they might have their house keys with them, which we won't be able to get if they are both stuck down a hole.

We make the meeting point at their house and set up

a trip wire. When they fall over it, we jump out and put a big blanket over them so they can't see. Then we tie them up in the blanket so they can't escape.

We go round to their house when they are in, slip a note under the door saying we have the passport and to meet us in the shed at the bottom of the garden. When they go into the shed, we lock the door and trap them in there. Whilst they are trapped inside, we can go and look in their house.

We thought this last idea might just work. When we were finished, we could escape through the back fence. We went to check whether we could lock the shed and discovered it has one of those locks that you pull a piece of metal across and put a padlock through it. It doesn't have a padlock on it at the moment, but we can easily get one. Then all we have to do before we escape is open the padlock. Hopefully, with it opened, they will be able to loosen it off by pushing the door so that they can get out once we're gone.

Now to make the note…

Barry and Shona we have something you are looking for If you want it back meet us in your shed tonight at 10 p.m.

FRIDAY

We posted the note through Barry and Shona's front door and then got to work making stick mirrors so when we're hiding in the bushes we'll be able to see when they come out of their house towards the shed. We decided not to take our walkie-talkies with us as they make a beeping noise every time you finish talking and release the button.

James came up with the idea of blackening our faces so we can't be seen in the bushes.

'No way am I doing that,' Stacey said.

James and I laughed.

'What do you think we're going to use – mud? Dog poo?' I said.

'I am going to be sick,' said Stacey.

'Don't be an idiot, Stacey, we'll use face paint, of course.'

'I knew that,' Stacey said.

But judging by the look on her face, she was lying. She really did think we were going to put dirt on our faces for our disguise. Maybe spies did have to do that before face paint was invented, but luckily we don't. And luckily, I have some face paint because Mum bought me some for last Halloween. It has black and white, as well as red, and it also had really cool fake blood, but I used all that up.

We decided to use a fox noise to communicate with each other. We only needed to do it as a signal to go into action. It was my idea to use the fox noise, as the fox was the culprit of the missing washing: our very first case. I thought it might bring us good luck and we needed that if we didn't have my lucky underpants to rely on.

I wish I hadn't just written that. I've been trying really hard not to think about my bad luck without my pants. Sometimes I forget though.

We practised the fox call for ages. It's sort of like a baby crying. I thought I was best at doing it, but Stacey said she was. I don't know why she always has to disagree with everything I do; it's as though she likes arguing with me or something.

'James, you sound more like a wolf,' I said. 'And we don't have wolves around here. It will give us away.'

'No, I don't,' James said, but he practised some more anyway. In the end, he sounded more like a dog, which is better than a wolf, so I didn't say anything. We agreed I would make the first call (as I am the leader): the signal to get into position. James would answer next, as my deputy, then, as soon as Stacey did hers, we would jump out and lock Barry and Shona in the shed (hopefully).

I convinced Mum to let us sleep in the tent in the garden, so James and I got dressed in dark clothes and painted our faces black. Then we waited for Stacey to arrive. Her mum and dad were out and her granny was babysitting. Stacey said it would be easy to get out of the house as her granny is deaf and never goes and checks on them because she is too old to go up the stairs.

When Stacey arrived, James painted her face too. Stacey brought snacks, which was a good idea to give us energy for the mission. We were all ready to go. I picked up my backpack full of spy things.

At 10:00 p.m. on the dot, Barry and Shona stepped out of their back door and walked towards their shed. From my hiding spot, I gave the signal to get ready. James replied and when Stacey did her fox noise we jumped out behind Barry and Shona.

First, I threw my Spiderman net over their heads and they got all tangled up. Then we pushed them into the shed and padlocked the door. It all happened very fast and I couldn't believe that the first part of the plan had actually worked.

We ran into the house. James went first and stopped dead, causing Stacey and me to run right into the back of him. What we saw gave us all a big shock. There was another man in there. We were scared but the man seemed just as scared as we felt. He looked at us, threw down a large envelope he had in his hands and ran out of the door.

'Woah, I did not expect that!' James said. His eyes looked wide, like two full moons against his dark face.

Inside the envelope was a passport, a birth certificate and some money.

'Another passport, like the one Perky took from Barry,' Stacey said. 'We should take these with us.'

We looked around the house. Everywhere seemed normal, just like any other house, except this place was old and dirty. Upstairs was different, though. In one of the bedrooms were some machines, set out on a couple of desks that were in the room instead of a bed and other stuff you'd normally find. On the desk were loads of different passports, birth certificates and money. I took my camera out of my back pocket and snapped some photos, for evidence.

'Are they making these things or something?' I said. 'Looks like a mini factory in here.'

'I wonder who all these people are,' Stacey said, flicking through the passports.

'I've seen something like this on TV,' James said. 'When people can't get a passport the usual way, they pay loads of money to get a fake one. People must come to Barry and Shona to get a new identity.'

'This is big,' I said. 'We should get out of here now and go and tell the police or something. I don't like this one bit.'

We backed out of the room onto the landing and were just about to leave when we heard voices downstairs. It was Barry and Shona. They had escaped the shed. We were trapped upstairs.

We didn't know what to do.

'We should hide in here,' James said, pointing in to the next bedroom. We all scrambled to find somewhere.

James threw himself onto the floor and slid under the bed and I ran round the other side to get under as well.

'You can't come under here too,' James said.

'Shut up and move over,' I said. So we huddled there together trying to be as still as possible.

'I don't know where to go,' Stacey said.

'In the wardrobe,' James said. 'Quick!'

Stacey hid in the wardrobe and we all waited in anticipation of the moment either Shona or Barry would burst into the room looking for us. We knew they were going to be really mad.

Then the door flung open and banged against the wall. Barry's voice echoed around the room.

'Where are you, you horrible little so and sos?' he said.

I was trying hard to stay as still as possible, holding my breath and concentrating as hard as I could. Then I heard a sneeze.

'What was that? I knew you were hiding in here.'

It was Stacey. Barry had found her. I heard the wardrobe door open and Stacey coughing.

'Come here you. What do you think you are doing trying to lock us in the shed?' Barry said. 'Shona, I've got one of them,' he called. 'The others must be around here somewhere.'

Stacey shrieked as Barry dragged her out of the room.

'Don't kill me, I didn't mean to do it,' I heard her say.

James and I stayed in our positions. We didn't dare move. Once Barry had gone, I let go of the breath I was holding and whispered to James, 'What do we do now?

We can't leave Stacey here – we don't know what they'll do to her.'

'I know,' James said, 'but how are we going to get out of this room without them noticing?'

'We'll be able to hear where they are,' I said. 'We have to use all our spy skills to make sure we're not caught. And we have to come up with a plan to help Stacey.'

As slowly as we could manage, we slid out from under the bed. Then James poked his head out first to make sure the coast was clear (I said I would do it but there was no point as he was nearest to the door). We crept to the top of the landing and strained our ears to listen for where Barry, Shona and Stacey were. It wasn't difficult. We could hear shouting coming from a room downstairs.

'Did you find what you came looking for?' It was Shona, shouting. 'Who put you up to this?'

'You don't scare me,' Stacey said back.

Shona and Barry started laughing.

'Ha, this one's brave isn't she?' Shona said. 'We'll see how brave you are when we've finished with you, shall we?'

'So you found out our little secret then,' Barry said. 'What exactly were you going to do about it, tell the police? But why would they believe a stupid little girl like you? And besides, you've done us a favour. By the time they come round here we'll be long gone and no one will ever know what we've been doing.'

'The police will find you,' Stacey shouted. 'We know who you are.'

'Don't make me laugh; do you think these are our

real names?' Shona said. 'Do we look stupid? They'll never find us. We've been doing this for years and have never been caught. We're not about to let some rotten interfering kids change all that, are we?'

I was scared. James looked at me.

'What are we going to do?' I said to him. As leader, I should have been the one to come up with something, but I had nothing and that made me feel pathetic.

'You've got to go and get the police NOW,' James said. 'I'll stay here and keep them busy until you get back.'

I looked at him and could see he was scared too, but James had always been much braver than me. He was always the one to step forward and do things, whilst I hid behind him, making excuses why it wasn't me. Well it was time to end all that. Time that I stepped up to the mark.

'No, you go,' I said. 'I'll stay here to help Stacey. I know what to do.'

'Are you sure?' James said and I nodded, afraid that if I spoke he might realise that I wasn't at all OK. I didn't want him to worry.

'How am I going to get out?' he said.

'You can go through the kitchen into the back garden and out the escape route,' I said.

James nodded and we sneaked downstairs and crept along the hall. The door to the room where Barry and Shona were holding Stacey was open slightly and we could see their shadows flicking across the wall. We pressed our backs against the opposite wall and took the slowest steps possible to get past, scared the floor would creak and give us away.

In the kitchen, there were two doors, one leading out to the garden and a mystery one. I thought about the layout of the house and realised this mystery one was a door leading in to the garage. Whispering to James, I pointed to it.

'I think this door goes in to the garage. If I open it at the same time as you open the back door and let it bang shut, they'll think we've gone in there. Then I'm coming outside with you.'

'Aren't you going to stay here and distract them?' James said.

'Yes I am, but there's something outside I need,' I said. 'I'll think of a way to get back in.'

I sounded a lot braver than I felt. On the count of three, we opened the doors at the same time and then escaped into the garden. James ran down to the bottom and through the fence, leaving me hiding behind one of the bushes where we had crouched earlier waiting for Barry and Shona.

From my position by the bush in the garden, I could see Barry dash into the kitchen and fling open the garage door. After a few minutes, he came out looking puzzled. Then he checked around the kitchen and noticed the back door open. He stuck his head out, craning his neck to see if anyone was in the garden, at which point I crouched down to avoid being spotted and didn't see where he looked after that. After waiting for what seemed like forever, I heard the back door close as he returned inside the kitchen.

Behind the bush was the backpack I had brought with me and I emptied it all out to see what I could use.

There was a torch, some night vision goggles (which were toy ones, so they weren't that good), stink bombs, a fake tarantula, handcuffs and some rope. Shoving it all back into the bag, I crawled out from behind the bush.

Judging by the shadows and the lights, Barry, Shona and Stacey were in the front room, so, keeping low, I moved towards the house, avoiding the window where Barry and Shona were. Barry had left the back door unlocked so I pushed down the handle and pulled it towards me, hoping it wouldn't creak. When the door opened just enough for me to get through, I squeezed through the gap and into the kitchen. I could hear Barry talking in the next room.

'We're going to have to get out of here in case the cops come,' he said. 'We'll have to take the girl with us and drop her off somewhere.'

'We can't take her, that's kidnap,' Shona said. 'This isn't what we do; it wasn't part of the plan.'

'Plans can change, Sho,' Barry said, 'and thanks to this one we have to change ours. She'll be all right.'

I had to act fast, so went to the garage hoping to find what I needed. I was in luck. In the garage was the main switch for the electricity. I knew all about it because I had seen my dad flick it when we had to turn the power off at our house. I got the rope out of the bag and set it up to stretch tightly behind the door, across the entrance to the garage, then I put on my night vision goggles.

After flicking the switch to cut the power, everything happened so fast. Barry and Shona started shouting and Stacey screamed. I knew Barry would try to find his way into the kitchen towards the garage and when he did he opened the door and tripped head first over the rope I'd set up. Because it was pitch black he wasn't able to see a thing and he fell straight onto the lawn mower and knocked himself out. I put the handcuffs on him just in case, grabbed the rope and then dashed out of the garage.

'Barry, is that you? What's happening?' I heard Shona shout out.

I stayed silent and crept towards the door where Shona had Stacey. Then I crushed a stink bomb and rolled it under the door. The door opened and she came out coughing and spluttering. Shona ran to the downstairs bathroom to be sick and Stacey tried to feel her way around, but she kept banging in to the wall. I ran to help her.

'Stacey, it's me, Harry. Here, take this,' I said, giving her the torch.

'Quick, let's shut her in the bathroom,' Stacey said, rushing to the door and holding it shut.

Inside, Shona started screaming. 'Let me out of here, you idiot!'

The two of us stood with our backs to the door trying to stop Shona from getting out.

'We have to get something to bar the door,' Stacey said. 'Can you hold her in whilst I go look?'

'Yes, go,' I said and pushed with all my strength.

Stacey came back dragging a chair from the dining room and we propped it at an angle under the door handle.

'We need to get something else to hold it,' she said.

So, together, we moved a hall table from behind the front door and added it to the other things. Shona was banging and pushing at the door from inside.

'Do you think it will hold?' Stacey said.

'I don't know, she's strong,' I said, as the door banged. We both jumped.

'If we could see, we could find some more stuff to prop against it,' Stacey said.

'That was me, I turned the lights off to get Barry to come in to the garage,' I said, explaining to Stacey what had happened.

'Nice work,' she said. 'but do you think you could turn them back on?'

'I know I can,' I said 'and it would be a good idea to check on Barry anyway. You stay here and make sure that Shona doesn't get out.'

I went back to the kitchen and into the garage. It was quiet and Barry was still on the floor. I went to the fuse box and switched the electricity back on. The garage was still dark but there was light coming from the kitchen. Suddenly Barry moved his head and began to moan. He turned and saw me.

'You…' he said. 'I'm going to kill you.'

He started to get up, so I ran out of the garage and slammed the door, holding it shut with all my weight.

'Stacey,' I shouted. Now we were both trapping someone in.

Stacey came into the kitchen.

'Barry's in here. I knocked him out but now he's come round. What can we do?'

Stacey looked around and then she ran towards something.

'What's this?' she said, grabbing a key hung by a string on the wall next to the garage door. 'It could be the key to the garage. Let me try it.'

Stacey put the key in the lock and it turned. We both breathed a sigh of relief. Then we heard the bathroom door banging.

'Quick, Shona is escaping,' I shouted.

When we got there, the door was partly open and Shona's hand was sticking through it. Stacey slammed the door shut right on to her hand. Shona screamed and I cringed, but was secretly impressed by Stacey's quick thinking. We got the door shut again and pushed the table and chair closer. Then we got other chairs from the dining room and piled them up outside the door.

'That should be enough to keep her in until the police get here,' I said.

'Have you phoned them?' Stacey said.

'No, but I helped James escape earlier, so he could go and get help,' I said. 'We just have to hang on now until they get here.'

So Stacey and I sat on the floor of the hallway listening to the sound of banging and shouting from both Barry and Shona and waiting until someone came to help. It seemed like we sat there for ages, until we heard different shouting and the sound of glass smashing in the kitchen. Stacey clutched my arm, moving closer. I could feel her shaking.

'What's that?' she said. 'Do you think Barry has got out? What should we do?'

But then we heard familiar voices.

'Where are you, what have you done with our kids?'

There was swearing too, so I'd better not repeat that.

'It's my dad and James' dad,' I said, jumping up.

'We're in here.'

I shouted back and the dads came barging into the hall where we had been crouching. My dad was holding a garden shovel and James' dad had a baseball bat. Both were holding their weapons in the air and looked battle-ready.

'Are you OK, kids?' Dad said, when he saw us. He looked around frantically, trying to make sense of the situation.

'We're fine, Dad. Everything is under control. Shona is in there and Barry is locked in the garage.'

'And you're not hurt?' Mr Murphy said, looking us over, turning Stacey and me this way and that.

'No we're fine, really,' Stacey said. 'Thank God you came though. We didn't know how long we could hold them here.'

'Don't worry, the police are on their way,' Dad said, as we heard the sound of sirens and saw the flashing of the police car lights outside the house.

★

When the police came in, I think they were surprised to find Stacey and me standing there with the two dads.

'Looks like you've done a great job without our help,' the police officer said.

Stacey and I looked at each other and beamed. It was the first time we have ever smiled at each other.

'But I think you need to go with one of our officers so they can take your statements. You've got some explaining to do.'

We both stopped smiling then, realising we were going to be in big trouble.

PART 5

What happened after James left Barry and Shona's house?

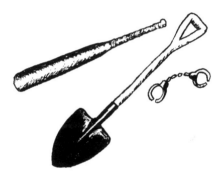

JAMES STORY

I thought it was best for James to fill in the details here, as he was the one who escaped and went to raise the alarm.

Oh boy, I am in so much trouble, I'm not sure if I will ever be able to leave my room again. This diary might be the only evidence I ever existed.

If you've ever said 'I think I'm going to die', you didn't know what you were talking about, because last night I really did think I was going to die.

I told Harry to escape so he could go and call the police, but he insisted I go, which isn't like him at all. I didn't want to leave him, but he seemed determined and one of us had to raise the alarm, so I escaped out of the hedge and ran home. All I could think about when I left was what would happen to him and Stacey. I thought about how brave Harry was as I stumbled down the back alleyway towards my house. I hoped he was brave enough to stay calm and do something to help Stacey. I knew it was my job to make sure I got help as fast as possible. This was a dangerous situation. It wasn't fun anymore and the secret agency no longer seemed like a good idea.

When I burst in through the kitchen door, it slammed against the cupboards behind it so hard that it made Mum and Dad come rushing into the kitchen to see what was going on. For a minute, I just stood there. The words wouldn't come out of my mouth.

'James, what's wrong?' Mum said, coming over towards me.

I know when Harry reads this bit I will never live it down, it's so embarrassing, but here goes – I cried, actually cried, and then told Mum and Dad what we had done.

'You have to call the police, Mum,' I said. 'Barry and Shona are crazy and they've got Stacey. I don't know what they're going to do to her, but they're really mad about what we did.'

Dad grabbed the phone and made the call.

'Tell them to hurry up,' I shouted.

'They'll get here as soon as they can, don't worry,' Mum said.

'I'm not waiting around for them to get here,' Dad said and he dashed out towards the garden.

'Dad, what are you doing?' I said, as he rushed past me, holding a shovel and a baseball bat he must have taken from the shed.

'You stay here with your mother,' Dad said, in a firm tone that meant if I disobeyed I would be in for it. 'I'm going to get those kids.'

'David, be careful, you don't know what they might do,' Mum said, holding me back, but Dad wasn't listening. We watched him march out of the door, greeted by an equally determined-looking Mr Smith and the pair marched towards number 35.

He must have called him too.

Knowing that the police were on their way and the two dads were going to the rescue should have made me feel better, but it didn't. I felt sick and couldn't stop pacing up and down the front room, looking out of the window and waiting for the sirens of the police cars. When they arrived, I relaxed a little and ran out to follow them. Mum called after me to stop, but I ignored her. I heard her swear and come running after me.

I ran all the way down to number 35 and straight into a police officer who was blocking the entrance to the gate.

'My friends are in there, and my dad, I need to go see if they're OK,' I said to him.

'You can't go in until the area has been declared safe,' he said.

'But are they going to be all right?'

The officer looked at me, as though he was about to tell me to stop whining and go home, then he seemed to change his mind.

'I'll radio through to find out,' he said and turned away from me.

Mum caught up with me then and put her hands on my shoulders, giving me a squeeze. By now, the noise and the lights from the police cars had brought a few of the neighbours out of their houses to see what was going on. I could hear Mrs O'Connor's Irish accent as she said 'I knew there was something fishy going on with that pair.' I didn't turn around though, just kept my eyes fixed on the house and the police officer still on his radio, my fingers crossed, willing everything to be all right.

When the policeman turned around, he started telling everyone to move back. Other police officers appeared to help clear the area.

'What's happening? Where is everyone?' I said to the one who was trying to shove me away.

'You're a friend of those two little wannabe detectives, are you?' he said.

I nodded, wanting to say we're actually secret agents, not detectives, and would there be a reward, but thought I'd better not in case I got arrested or something.

'Well, I don't know whether to call them idiots or heroes, but they've certainly done us a favour by catching hold of these two.'

'They're OK, then?'

'Yes, a little shaken up, but otherwise fine. They'll be out in a minute. That's quite a job they did in there.'

Relief turned to jealousy as I wondered what Harry and Stacey had done. Part of me wanted to tell him I was the third man, but something told me he wouldn't be impressed, so I kept my mouth shut.

I watched as Barry and Shona were led away out of number 35's gate and into one of the waiting cars. They both had their hands cuffed behind their back.

Stacey and Harry followed, with Dad and Mr Smith. They weren't handcuffed, which was a relief, and they both looked fine – apart from their blackened faces, which were a bit smudged. Stacey's parents had just arrived home from their night out and came to see what all the fuss was about. When Stacey saw them, she ran over. Harry's mum joined him and his dad in a group hug.

'Come on,' Dad said, coming over to Mum and me, 'let's get you home. You've got a lot of explaining to do, starting with why you've all got black faces and why you were hanging around this house.'

PART 6

How I escaped my kidnappers, by Stacey Webster

STACEY'S STORY

I think you know by now what Stacey is like and as you can imagine there was no way she was going to let me complete this story without adding her bit to it.

I knew as soon as James and Harry hid under the bed I was in trouble. There was nowhere for me to hide that wasn't obvious. I mean, under a bed is quite obvious when you think about it, but Barry or Shona were bound to find me first.

There was also another problem. The wardrobe was full of cobwebs and when I felt one tickle my nose I couldn't help it, I sneezed. That was when Barry found me. He dragged me out of the wardrobe and started shouting.

My first thought was that he would kill me. I really did think I might never see my family again and tried so hard not to cry. That thought made me get mad though. If I was going to die, I might as well die fighting, and I wasn't going to let them know how scared I really was.

Barry was fat and had a beard. I hadn't looked at him more closely before, but when he pulled me down the stairs and into the living room I got a good look at him.

I thought it would be a good idea to do that in case I did get out of there alive and needed to give the police a description. Fat, hairy and stinky he was, but, underneath all that hair, I thought he actually wasn't that old. Not as old as my dad anyway.

Shona was young too. She had long dark brown hair, parted in the middle and hanging around her face. There were braids in her hair and she wore a kind of thin headband that sat across her forehead. She was quite pretty really, but in that moment I hated them both.

As they argued about what to do with me, I looked around to see if there was any way I could escape. They'd left the door to the living room open and I was just about to make a dash for it when all the lights went off. It was so black I literally couldn't see a thing, like being blind. It was my best chance to get out, but just as I was about to move towards the door Barry barged into me and knocked me down. He pulled me back up and shoved me towards Shona, who managed to grab my arms and hold them behind my back. I wriggled to break free but she was surprisingly strong.

Barry swore a lot as he banged and crashed his way towards the door. He was going to try to turn the lights back on I think. That was when I heard another loud crash and I didn't know until after that it was Harry capturing Barry. I didn't even know Harry was there at all until the stink bomb rolled into the room.

Now, I'm used to that smell but obviously Shona wasn't. She let go of me and started coughing and making sick noises. She stumbled towards the door and left me there. I tried to make my way out too, but it was impossible in the darkness. I kept banging into the wall. It was such a relief to bump into Harry. He gave me a torch and together we trapped Shona in the bathroom.

★

It was only afterwards, when it was all over, that I got really scared about what could have happened to us. Mum said it was delayed shock. Both my parents cried when they found out what had gone on. They'd just come home after their night out and said they came to see what all the neighbours were crowding in the street for and why the police were there. Imagine their surprise when they saw Barry and Shona in handcuffs, followed by Harry and me with blackened faces. I felt bad for making them so upset, but the next day they got mad, so I guess they got over it quickly.

I was officially grounded for the rest of the holidays, just like the boys. It wasn't so bad though. I'd enjoyed being part of Harry's secret agency and I'm glad we solved the mystery of number 35. It was all kind of worth it in the end. I mean, we were OK, weren't we? We caught some criminals, didn't we? Plus, we did something amazing in the summer holidays and I bet no one can match that. I can't wait to go back to school and I don't think I've ever said that in my life.

PART 7

Final word from me
(Agent Harry Bond)

Barry and Shona, it turns out, were wanted criminals who had been moving around the country for years, calling themselves by different names so they wouldn't get caught. They were part of an underground operation producing false identities for people such as criminals or anyone who was staying in the country illegally. They made passports, birth certificates and all sorts of other papers you need to pretend to be another person. Plus, they even made fake money.

They pretended to move into number 35, but never stayed there at all. Instead, they came to the house every night, bringing with them a person who wanted something, like a passport, so they could do the deal. Then they would drive back to wherever they came from. I suppose they did that so the person they did business with would never be able to find them.

Barry and Shona didn't count on us being around though, did they? And it was our job as secret agents to work out what they were up to. We found out their secret and caught them in the act. Yeah, I know it went a bit wrong and we could have got into serious trouble, but we still managed to catch them and keep them locked up until the police arrived (Stacey and I did anyway). If I'd known who they were, I'm not sure if I would have been brave enough to stay behind at the house, though. And thinking about it now, I still can't believe I did that.

You would think the police would be grateful, but they're just as cross with us as our parents are. Perhaps they're jealous because we caught them and they didn't. I overheard an officer saying they'd been after Barry and Shona for a long time, so I guess the police felt a bit silly that a bunch of kids managed to do what they couldn't.

James asked for a reward (typical James) and they said 'no chance'.

So that was it: four weeks of madness, followed by getting into loads of trouble. Mum and Dad went from shouting to hugging me, to giving me praise for a job well done and then to calling me an idiot for getting into that situation in the first place. I don't think they knew what to think, but they said 'no more trouble from now on'. I guess that's it for the secret agency then: closed down by senior officials (our parents) for health and safety reasons (because we all nearly got caught by Barry and Shona and they are still freaking out).

Maybe that's not a bad thing. The mission is complete and so the agents are happy to retire.

Besides, I can't see James or Stacey anyway because they're grounded too. I don't know what will happen now. Two mysteries are probably enough for one small street. And besides, we go back to school next week. Boo hoo...

Talking of mysteries, there is one final one I still haven't got to the bottom of, and that is

WHAT HAPPENED TO MY LUCKY UNDERPANTS
(bottom of – get it?!).

You won't believe this. Even though I played so badly during the holiday football camps, I still got picked for the team to play in the pre-season cup. Coach said he was giving me a second chance because he knew I didn't usually play like that and I'd better not let him down.

As if that wasn't pressure enough, I almost thought about not playing at all. I knew I would be rubbish without my lucky underpants. Not having them had brought me so much bad luck this summer. Yes, we may have uncovered some serious criminals, but the danger we'd got ourselves into in order to catch Barry and Shona could have got us killed.

It was Max, of all people, who convinced me to play.

'You don't need any lucky pants,' he said.

I tried to tell him otherwise but he put up his hand to stop me, giving me that look, you know, the one that your mum gives you sometimes (who does he think he is?).

'I know you think you need them, but I promise you, you'll be fine. You're a good little player and you won't hear me say that very often, perhaps never again, you got that?'

I could only nod back at him. I mean, my brother, giving me praise? That's unheard of. I was about to smile, but thought I'd better not.

'Just get out there and play like you always do. Imagine you have those lucky pants if you need to, but don't think about the fact you don't have them.'

I thought that was good advice, actually: pretend I'm wearing them. It could work and I was prepared to give it a shot. I also thought about that night at Barry and Shona's house. If I could be brave enough to catch wanted criminals, perhaps I could play a football game without my lucky pants.

My brother walked off and then ignored me for the rest of the day. I found myself wondering whether he had actually said that to me at all or if I'd just imagined it.

The advice was good though. On the day of the game, I told myself I was wearing my lucky underpants and I was going to play brilliantly. Guess what? I did. My defending could go down in legend history, my dad said, like John Terry or Ashley Cole. What was even more impressive was I scored the winning goal – me, a defender!

It was 1:1 with minutes to go. Our team were pushing and attacking but we just couldn't get through the other team's defence. All eleven men were forward. One mistake and we'd have been completely open at the back and in big trouble. Olly, our right midfielder, crossed the ball. I was in the middle, outside the box, and when the ball connected with my foot, I volleyed it straight into the top corner. Seconds later, the ref blew his whistle and the crowd went mental. I was the hero and it felt amazing.

★

That night the weirdest thing happened. I pulled back my duvet to get into bed and what do you think was there? My lucky underpants! There they were, under the covers as if they'd been there all along. I couldn't believe it. I'd looked everywhere for those pants (as you know) and I've slept in my bed loads of times since I'd lost them.

But two things have happened recently:

My mum changed my duvet cover.

My brother was made to clean out his room because it was so gross in there.

Mum swears she didn't see the pants when she was changing the bed covers, and my brother completely denies he had them in his room all along but just didn't know it because it was so messy in there. So who is telling the truth?

The disappearing underpants may have been found, but as to how they disappeared, well, I guess that's still a mystery. Do you know what though? It doesn't matter anymore because now I know I don't need them.

About the Author

Nikki Young is a children's fiction author and writing tutor. She lives in Kent with her husband, three children and their Boston Terrier dog and is the author of 'The Mystery of the Disappearing Underpants' and the 'Time School' Series.

On a mission to get children writing, Nikki runs Storymakers, a creative writing club for children aged 7 and above, which provides weekly writing groups, holiday workshops and 1:1 tuition and mentoring.

Find out more at www.nikkiyoung.co.uk

Follow her on Twitter: @nikki_cyoung
Instagram: @nikkiyoungwriter
Facebook.com/nikkiyoungwriter

Printed in Great Britain
by Amazon